T0020664

# Seashells by the Seashore

By Marianne Berkes
Illustrated by Robert Noreika

Dawn Publications

Sue walks along the seashore
warmed by the sun.
Picking up seashells one by one.

Here's a pretty Periwinkle.
What a work of art!

Let's find some more shells;
We're off to a good start.

Periwinkle

Kitten's Paw

Seashells tumble
From the ocean blue.

Find a tiny Kitten's Paw
So Sue can have two.

Periwinkle

Kitten's Paw

Jingle Shell

Once creatures lived
In these shells from the sea.

Here's a fragile Jingle Shell.
Now there are three.

Periwinkle
Kitten's Paw
Jingle Shell
Olive Shell

*When the animals die,*
*The shells wash up to shore.*

*A smooth and empty Olive Shell*
*Will bring us up to four.*

Periwinkle

Kitten's Paw

Jingle Shell

Olive Shell

Scallop Shell

*We're getting good at "shelling."*
*No time to swim or dive.*

*A Scallop has a fan shape—*
*That makes five!*

So many seashells
That we can mix.

If we find a Whelk Shell
There will be six.

Periwinkle
Kitten's Paw
Jingle Shell
Olive Shell
Scallop Shell
Whelk Shell
Oyster Shell

*How the seashells glisten*
*In the sun that shines from heaven.*

*Here's a bumpy Oyster Shell*
*So that makes seven.*

Periwinkle
Kitten's Paw
Jingle Shell
Olive Shell
Scallop Shell
Whelk Shell
Oyster Shell
Slipper Shell

The tide is rolling in
And it's getting pretty late.

This shell looks like a slipper!
Now we have eight.

We're scouring through the beach sand.
Lots of shells are fine.

We want to find a Moon Shell
To bring us up to nine!

"I've got some really awesome shells"
Sue tells her brother, Ben

He's found a spiny pen shell.
Now there are ten.

"Do you think she'll like them?"
Ben asks Sue.

"Grandma walked this beach, Ben,
Just like me and you.

"She loved to look for different shells
Of every shape and size.

"And so these treasures that we've found
Will be a great surprise."

Periwinkle
Kitten's Paw
Jingle Shell
Olive Shell
Scallop Shell
Whelk Shell
Oyster Shell
Slipper Shell
Moon Shell
Pen Shell
Ark Shell

"I've got one too!"
Says Ben's friend, Evan.

He adds a heavy Ark Shell
And that makes eleven.

Periwinkle
Kitten's Paw
Jingle Shell
Olive Shell
Scallop Shell
Whelk Shell
Oyster Shell
Slipper Shell
Moon Shell
Pen Shell
Ark Shell
Cockle Shell

They'll scrub the seashell sculptures
To put on Grandma's shelves.

Let's find a Cockle Shell
So there will be twelve.

Twelve seashell treasures
Are in Sue's pail.

But wait! What's this?
A slimy sea snail?

That's the mollusk inside,
Alive as it can be.

We need to take him down
To his home in the sea.

Evan takes the Whelk Shell
Down to the shore.

The creature living deep inside
Will crawl around once more.

"Happy Birthday, Grandma!
And many, many more.

We have a special gift for you—
Seashells from the seashore."

Shell sculptures are some of the most incredible designs in nature. There are many kinds. In this story some are large and some are small. Others are long or round, and some are bumpy or smooth. Some are even named for what they look like.

Seashells are made by the animals that live inside them. These sea creatures are called mollusks. A mollusk has a soft body that needs protection from a hard shell.

Most of the shells found on the beach can be put into two groups. One group is called "univalves." "Uni" means "one," so they have only one shell. Univalves are mollusks that move on one foot. Periwinkles, olive shells and whelks are part of this group.

The second group is called "bivalves." "Bi" means two. The mollusk lives between the two parts of this double shell, which is joined by a hinge. When the shell is open, it can eat by taking food from the water. When danger threatens, the two shells quickly snap shut. Oysters, scallops and ark shells are part of this group.

Turn the page for a description of the shells that are in this book. Can you name the univalves and the bivalves? Which ones are smooth or bumpy? Which ones are named for what they look like? Next time you go to the beach, look for these shells, or other favorites, to put in your bucket. Collect only empty shells; never remove live mollusks from their homes. It is a good idea to scrub the shells in warm, soapy water. Once they have been cleaned, they can be beautifully displayed.

***Periwinkles*** *have a distinctive shape. Most of them come to a point and have banded lines around them. This univalve lives in marshes and on rocks, and can live out of water longer than other sea creatures. The empty shells found on beaches can be smooth or prickly.*

***Kitten Paws*** *are small bivalves whose shells look like a paw. After a long time in the sun, they fade to a lustrous white. Usually half of the shell washes up on the beach, while the other half remains attached to rocks or other shells with a powerful glue the mollusk makes.*

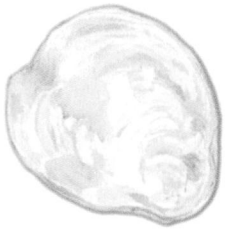

***Jingle Shells*** *are thin bivalves that you can see through. The top shell, which is cupped and pearly, washes ashore more often than the lower shell. There is a hole in the lower shell where the animal anchors itself. People string these shells together to make wind chimes that tinkle.*

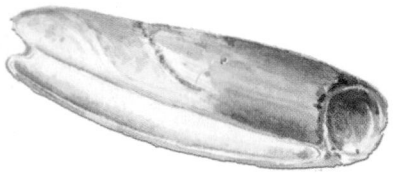

***Olive Shells*** *are smooth and glossy because the mollusk wraps its soft body, commonly called its foot, around the shell and keeps it polished. It is a univalve that is long and shaped like a tube. Some olive shells have greenish gray with reddish brown zigzag markings. These are called 'lettered' shells. They are usually found buried in the sand.*

***Scallop Shells*** *usually have unequal bivalves. The lower one is raised while the upper one is flat with beautiful colors. The calico scallop, which has equal bivalves, can be a mixture of white, rose, purple, brown and yellow-orange with many ribs running from the hinge to the outer edge.*

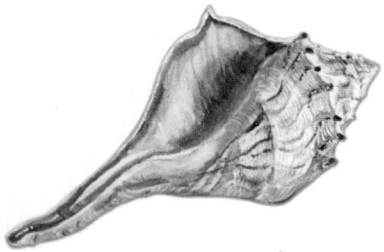

***Whelk Shells*** *are moderately large univalves that can be found alive in shallow waters and mud flats. They have a solid shell that narrows to a long pointy open canal. The shell sculpture is somewhat varied. A whelk is a sea snail that stretches out a big foot that it crawls around on.*

***Oyster Shells*** *are unequal bivalves that are large and heavy. They are easy to identify because they resemble elongated feet. The rough and bumpy shells are usually long and somewhat curved, and vary in shape depending on how and where they lived. Many people use this mollusk as a source for food.*

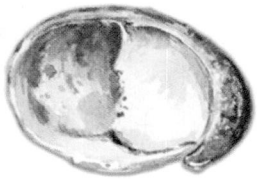

***Slipper Shells*** *are found among rocks and on other shells in shallow water. You might also see them attached to each other in a pile. A thin shelf covers half of the shell like the top of a slipper. That is how this cup-shaped, light-colored univalve with tan spots got its name.*

***Moon Shells*** *are snails that feed on other univalves. They are found burrowed in the sand at low tide. Shiny and smooth, their violet and brown color tends to fade when the shells wash ashore. On top of the shell there is a beautiful swirl with an eye in the middle.*

***Pen Shells*** *are large delicate brown bivalves. They have at least 15 rows of tubular spines that look like a fan. Other sea creatures sometimes attach themselves to the dead shells so when you first see them on the beach, they may look ugly. But the inside looks like mother-of-pearl.*

***Ark Shells*** *are a type of clam. These bivalves are heavy and have many ribs. These strong shells sometimes attach themselves to the undersides of rocks. One kind of ark shell, the cut-ribbed ark, is long and has a dark mossy coating. But after it has tumbled around in the surf, it is often pure white when it washes up on the beach.*

***Cockle Shells*** *are bivalves that vary in size from 1/2 inch to 5 inches. They look like a heart when they are closed—nature's own valentine. The inside usually is a beautiful purple or pink. These shells are often used for ashtrays and small containers.*

**Marianne Berkes** has spent much of her life as a teacher, children's theater director and children's librarian. She knows how much children enjoy "interactive" stories and is the author of nine entertaining and educational picture books that make a child's learning relevant. Reading, music and theater have been a constant in Marianne's life. Her books are also inspired by her love of nature. She hopes to open kids' eyes to the magic found in our natural world. Marianne now writes full time. She also visits schools and presents at conferences. She is an energetic presenter who believes that "hands on" learning is fun. Her website is www.MarianneBerkes.com.

**Robert Noreika** is a watercolorist with a passion for nature and art. He attended the Paier College of Art in Hamden, Connecticut and has his studio in an Arts Center in Avon, Connecticut. He has always loved to comb the beaches and hike in woods, and now he does so with his wife, Chris, and daughter, Sarah. This is the fourth book he has illustrated. His paintings hang in both corporate and private collections throughout the United States, Europe, and Japan.

## OTHER BOOKS BY MARIANNE BERKES

**The "Over" Series** features baby animals in their unique habitats. By using song, counting, and action words, Marianne has created wonderfully engaging books for early learners.

*Over in the Grasslands: On an African Savanna*

*Over on a Desert: Somewhere in the World*

*Over in the Ocean: In a Coral Reef*

*Over in the Jungle: A Rainforest Rhyme*

*Over in the Arctic: Where the Cold Winds Blow*

*Over in a River: Flowing Out to the Sea* (10 American rivers)

*Over in Australia: Amazing Animals Down Under*

*Over in the Forest: Come and Take a Peek*

*Over on a Mountain: Somewhere in the World* (Global)

*Baby on Board: How Animals Carry Their Young* — Tucked in pouches, gripped in teeth, propped on back, or underneath—these are just some of the cleaver ways animals carry their babies.

*Going Home: The Mystery of Animal Migration* — A fascinating, inspiring look at animals that migrate "home," often over great distances.

*What's in the Garden?* — Guess what food this is? Plus here are a few tasty recipes to start a lifetime of good eating.

## OTHER BOOKS FROM DAWN PUBLICATIONS

*Salmon Stream* — Fast-paced prose and brilliant illustrations follow the salmon from eggs in a stream to the wide ocean, eventually coming to their home stream.

*A Swim through the Sea* — This alphabet and alliteration book is a classic introduction to the marine habitat, illustrated and written by a 16 year-old.

*Kiki's Reef* — A baby green sea turtle scrambling on a beach eventually becomes the gentle giant of a coral reef. Here is an eye-opening tale of the circle of life.

*Granny's Clan: A Tale of Wild Orcas* — Life as a wild killer is very much a family affair. This clan is led by Granny, a 100 year-old matriarch who teaches young ones the art of survival.

*Octopus Escapes Again* — Swim along with Octopus as she searches for food and outwits dangerous enemies by using a dazzling display of defenses. Oh, yes, Octopus escapes again and again!

*A Moon of My Own* — An adventurous young girl journeys around the world, if only in her dreams. She discovers natural beauty and man-made wonders, accompanied by her companion—the moon.

*The Prairie that Nature Built* — A wild prairie is a lively place in this rhythmic romp with munchers and crunchers on the plain.

Dawn Publications is dedicated to inspiring in children a deeper understanding and appreciation for all life on Earth. To view our full list of titles or to order, please visit our web site at www.dawnpub.com, or call 800-545-7475.

# Seashells from the Seashore

## As Seen in the Book

# Seashells from the Seashore

## Other Common Shells